SUPER HAPPY PARTY BEARS

TiNY PRANCER

SUPER
HAPPY
PARTY
BEARS

TiNY PRANCER

MARCIE
COLLEEN

【Imprint】
MAKE YOUR MARK
NEW YORK

[Imprint]
MAKE YOUR MARK

A part of Macmillan Publishing Group, LLC
175 Fifth Avenue, New York, NY 10010

Library of Congress Control Number: 2016962163

ISBN 978-1-250-12414-2 (trade paperback) / ISBN 978-1-250-12415-9 (ebook)

Our books may be purchased in bulk for promotional, educational, or
business use. Please contact your local bookseller or the Macmillan
Corporate and Premium Sales Department at (800) 221-7945 ext. 5442
or by e-mail at MacmillanSpecialMarkets@macmillan.com.

Book design by Christine Kell
Imprint logo designed by Amanda Spielman
Illustrations by Steve James

First Edition—2017

1 3 5 7 9 10 8 6 4 2

mackids.com

If this book isn't yours, keep your thieving paws off it.
Obey or may you get decked in the hall by the holly.

TO MY READERS.
I CELEBRATE YOU.

CHAPTER ONE

Welcome to the Grumpy Woods!

'Tis the season before the Great Hibernation. A season of kindness. A season of goodwill and cheer. A season to gather with loved ones. So, grab anything jolly and joyous and jingle all the way—back where you came from!

That's right. Scoot, before Sheriff

Sherry hauls you off to City Hall.

You do not want to be fined for

unlawful tinsel tails or yule yaks.

This time of year, it's quiet time.

Perfect for a long winter's nap.

Now don't go misunderstanding.

It's not that all the critters in the

Grumpy Woods are hibernators. It's just that everyone needs a break occasionally. Being grumpy can be extremely exhausting, and the townscritters like to have some downtime. And what better season to curl up and enjoy some solitude than winter?

But the townscritters just
don't like all the hoopla of the
pre-hibernation holiday season.
They would rather skip it and
head straight for bed. They don't
understand the need to gather
together and celebrate before the
big sleep.

Why? you ask.

Perhaps their crankypants are too tight.

Perhaps their tails aren't screwed on just right.

It could be that they are simply GRUMPY! Stop trying to analyze it. Just scram!

This past year has been tough on the critters in the Grumpy Woods. Between chipmunk and squirrel rumbles, unruly pet caterpillars, and a constant array of intruders—from honeybees to punk bats—it's been one disaster after another. The last thing the townscritters want to do is have another party.

Every year is the same. Just as the townscritters are fluffing their pillows and curling up for some well-deserved rest, the Super Happy Party Bears parade in to

"Bring More Yay to the Holiday!"
The bears lift their voices in a
chorus of merriment while pulling
wagons full of shiny-wrapped
presents and holiday treats. The
bears' gifts are always too loud, too
colorful, and downright useless!

Last year Mayor Quill held an official meeting at City Hall. (City Hall is really just an upturned log, not actually a hall of any sort.)

The Super Happy Party Bears were not invited to the meeting.

At that meeting, everyone—from

Squirrelly Sam to Dawn Fawn—
brainstormed a list of ways to stop
the bears' holiday partying.

Humphrey Hedgehog suggested
Operation Play Possum, in which all
the townscritters would pretend to
be asleep when the bears arrived

with their holiday haul. Everyone
grumbled about it, but no one had
a better idea. So they voted. That
was that. It was very official.

For days, the townscritters were
on edge, ready to "stop, drop,
and snore" the second the bears

11

showed up. The big moment came
during the last City Hall meeting of
the year. Just as Mayor Quill was
about to bang his gavel to bring
order to the room, the sound of
a dozen furry feet tugging wagon
after wagon of festive fun rolled up
outside.

By the time the bears entered City Hall, the critters were posed in slumber. But it didn't stop the bears. Instead, they decorated the snoozing pile of neighbors with tinsel, glittery pinecones, popcorn and cranberry garlands, and

twinkling lights. Lastly, they stacked presents around the townscritters, placed a plate of tasty treats beside each sleepyhead, and tiptoed out.

The townscritters weren't sure that the bears had left, so they remained that way for a long time. Eventually, they really did fall asleep and awoke several hours later with sprinkles and frosting stuck to their faces and tinsel pasted everywhere else. It took hours to untangle themselves from garlands and twinkle lights. They

looked like a
grouchy ball of
holiday spirit
gone horribly
wrong.

And so,
even today,
everyone in the Grumpy Woods
still wakes up with scraps of tinsel
stuck to their toes and orders up
some breakfast—a triple-decker
sauerkraut and toadstool sandwich
and a heaping spoonful of *Bah
humbug!*

That is, everyone except the
Super Happy Party Bears.

The Super Happy Party Bears
love the holiday season!

If you follow the carefully placed sticks, laid out in the shape of arrows, up the flower-lined path, you'll see a welcome sign. That's Party Patch, the Headquarters of Fun. Life there is very different. Life is super. LIFE IS HAPPY. Life is full of parties!

And so, every holiday, those jolly happy souls order up a feast—a bowlful of jelly that shakes when they laugh with an extra dash of *Fa-la-la-la-la!!*

Nothing annoys the critters of the Grumpy Woods more.

Except when the bears have a party.

And they are always having a party.

CHAPTER TWO

This year, the bears were planning
the biggest holiday yet. Every
inch of the Party Patch looked like
it had been hit by a blizzard—a
super jolly holiday blizzard. The
Super Happy Party Bears scurried
about, in and out of piles of
ornaments, clouds of sawdust,

and colorful bowls of this and that. To Squirrelly Sam, who spied through the window, it looked like utter chaos. But inside, everything was going exactly as planned.

First, the Decoration Committee made sure anything and everything within reach was glitter-glued and covered with ribbons and beads, then repurposed on a wreath or a bunch of twigs or strung into a garland. Some of the decorations would stay at the Party Patch, but many would be shared around the woods.

One year the bears created sparkly wind chimes out of salt- and pepper shakers. When the wind blew, a tinkling tune was accompanied by sprinkling salt to look like snow. However, the bears used both salt *and* pepper, which set off a lot of wheezing and sneezing from the townscritters—a chorus that the Super Happy Party Band cheerfully set to music.

Next, the Baking Committee was focused on frosting sheets of sugar cookies to look like their

Grumpy friends as other goodies
simmered, bubbled, and baked
in the kitchen. While Little Puff's
cookies looked remarkably lifelike,
the others were more artistic in
their interpretations.

Jacks held up a cookie he was

just finishing. "This is Mayor Quill after he ate a messy red lollipop."

"This is Opal Owl with Big Puff's hairdo," said Mops.

Once the cookie neighbors were completed, they would be placed in a gingerbread version of the woods, complete with pretzel-stick trees, a popcorn Grumpy Wall, and a Grumpy Bramble made from berries, of course.

Lastly, the rest of the bears took on perhaps the most important preparation of all: gift making!

Earlier they had gone house

to house in the Grumpy Woods

asking every townscritter what

they would like for the holiday.

In past years, the townscritters

would scoff and huff and refuse to engage in such silliness. But this year, to the bears' surprise, each townscritter quickly offered up a holiday wish. A few even smiled.

"Sheriff Sherry wants ssssockssss," the littlest bear read from the list.

"I wonder why," said Jigs. "She doesn't have any feet."

Bubs, the voice of party wisdom, was there to explain. "She meant a sock snake doll."

"Can you imagine anything cuter than Sheriff Sherry snuggled up with a sock snake?" sighed the littlest bear happily.

"Who wants to make a sock doll for Sherry?" asked Jigs, adding the word *snake* after *sock* on the list.

The littlest bear raised his paw. He was an expert at making friends out of socks.

Jigs continued to read. "Humphrey Hedgehog would like some new underwear. I'll do that. I have a new design for undies that make a sound like maracas when you walk."

Squirrelly Sam gasped, his nose pressed up against the window and his mouth wide open. He had seen and heard enough. Clearly, something had to be done to stop the holiday.

CHAPTER THREE

Sam arrived at City Hall just as the mayor was about to bring the meeting to a close.

"STOP!" yelled Sam, leaping across the tops of heads to get to the podium.

"Sam, just because you missed

the meeting doesn't mean you can barge in here—" lectured Mayor Quill.

"UNDERWEAR IS NO LONGER BORING!" blurted Sam from atop the podium. "And socks and fruitcake!" Sam referred to the list

of gift ideas the townscritters had given the bears.

This year, everyone agreed to ask for boring gifts in hopes they might stump the bears and take the fun out of the holiday. Perhaps

the lack of gifts would stop the celebration altogether. But Sam's snooping had revealed that this wasn't the case.

"What are you talking about?" asked Mayor Quill.

"They are making it *all*!" screamed Sam.

"WhoOOOO said frOOOOtcake?"

asked Opal. "It's a CAKE! The bears love cake."

"But it's gross cake!" defended Bernice. "What did *you* ask for?"

"An ugly sweater," said Opal.

"Oh, it's a regular knitting factory at Party Patch. Sweaters for us all!" shrieked Sam.

Frantic murmurs bubbled up from the gathered bunch.

"I don't look good in sweaters!"

"How can underwear not be boring?"

"I will not eat fruitcake."

"Please! Everyone! Order!" yelled Quill as he banged his gavel on the

podium. "No need to panic. Let's not give up hope. Surely they will be stumped by *some* of our wishes. I promise we will have a pleasant and peaceful pre-hibernation here in the Grumpy Woods."

"What did you asssssk for?" Sherry asked the mayor.

"A train with square wheels on its caboose," stated Mayor Quill proudly.

Bernice rolled her eyes. "You're right. Can't imagine them figuring that one out."

"But when they try to drive it over here," explained the mayor, "the caboose will drag and slow them down!"

City Hall erupted once more with alarm.

"We're dOOOOmed!"

"I won't eat fruitcake, either."

43

"We need a Plan B!"

At the mention of a Plan B, all eyes turned to Humphrey. He was usually chock-full of ideas and plans, complete with blueprints. Everyone waited.

"I told you before this was a bad idea," murmured Humphrey from his spot right next to Mayor Quill's podium.

"Well, Mr. I-Asked-for-Underwear, what do you propose we do?" snapped Mayor Quill.

"This year," said Humphrey smugly, "I have no time to waste on the Super Happy Party Bears. I will take my *real* holiday wish

directly to the source. The Grand Cranberry."

"The Grand Cranberry?"

"Whoever heard of the Grand Cranberry?"

"Are there cranberries in fruitcake?"

"The Grand Cranberry is a tart yet good-willed soul," explained Humphrey. "And every year on Hibernation Eve, he rises from the Grumpy Bog and floats through the air with his bags of presents for everyone."

"Good grief," said Mayor Quill.
"Believing in a magical gift-bearing
berry? That's your plan?"

"If you will excuse me, sir," said
Humphrey, "I must prepare for the
Grand Cranberry's arrival. While
you are all sitting around in your

ugly sweaters eating fruitcake, I plan to get what I really want this holiday season."

With a *harrumph*, Humphrey turned to exit, and the townscritters erupted into a fit of giggles.

CHAPTER FOUR

Before Humphrey turned the
doorknob to leave, there came a
knock.

KNOCK, KNOCK, KNOCK!

"Maybe it's King Kumquat,"
laughed Bernice Bunny.

"Or the Royal Raissssin,"
chortled Sherry.

51

Humphrey did not laugh.

But when Mayor Quill opened the door, his smile quickly disappeared. Standing in a horseshoe were the Super Happy Party Bears wearing mittens and knit caps. They beamed from ear to ear. Jacks stood at the center holding a sign.

"WHOOOO is it?" asked Opal.

Jacks turned the sign around
to reveal the words TELL THEM IT'S
CAROL SINGERS.

"It's carol singers," answered
Mayor Quill, clenching his teeth.
The rest of the townscritters
gathered around.

Tunes hit PLAY on her boom box, and all the bears began to sing about snowflakes and sugarplums and kindness and cheer.

"Oh, the noise! Oh, the noise! Noise! Noise! Noise!" complained the townscritters while covering their ears.

The bears thought it was a new dance move and covered their ears, too. Which caused them to sing louder.

"IT'S SUPER HAPPY JOLLY TIME! SUPER HAPPY JOLLY TIME!" the bears chanted, doing their Super Happy Party Dance.

Slide to the right.

Hop to the left.

Shimmy, shimmy, shake.

Strike a pose.

In a grand finale, a party cannon launched confetti into the air. The tiny pieces of paper fell gently like snow all over the doorstep of City Hall and covered the townscritters.

"Happy Holiday," the bears said, thrusting a glitter-covered flyer into the mayor's paws before skipping back toward the Party Patch. "See you at the party!"

"Just wait until you taste the fruitcake!" announced Little Puff before she was quickly shushed by the others. After all, holiday presents were meant to be secrets.

Mayor Quill looked closely at the flyer. It was an invitation.

It's the most wonderful time of the year and you're invited!

PARTY PATCH HIBERNATION EVE

Mayor Quill stomped his foot.
He shook from head to toe. The
townscritters took cover just
as quills exploded everywhere.
Several quills soared straight into

the mountains of confetti, causing another scattering. One last quill zoomed straight for Humphrey. He threw his hands up, screamed, and dove into the pile.

When the quill storm had passed, Humphrey popped his head out of the heap he was hiding in. He looked around at the confetti-covered City Hall.

"It looks like a blizzard hit," said Humphrey.

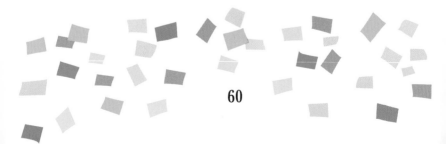

Mayor Quill trembled with anger.

"We're about to be buried under a blizzard of musical underwear and square-wheeled trains!" screamed Sam.

Humphrey nervously cleared his throat. "Statistically, a snowy holiday is a common wish. Though it seems a tad warm for it this year."

Everyone threw icy stares at Humphrey.

The hedgehog chattered on to fill the angry silence. "The

clear weather is nice for all the
families traveling to be together for
Hibernation Eve. In fact, when I was

just a baby my great-aunt Bridget

got stuck for three whole days in

a nasty blizzard on her way to our

house. My mother cried into her

figgy pudding."

"I wish a big ssssnowssssstorm

would bury the Party Patch,"

hissed Sherry. "Then sssssee them try to sssselebrate the holiday."

"SNOW WOES! SNOW WOES!" sang Dawn Fawn, frantically trying to sweep up the confetti mess.

"That's it!" declared Bernice. "We need snow!"

"We can't *make* it snow," complained Sam.

"I know someone who can," said Humphrey.

CHAPTER FIVE

"I am *not* writing a letter to a cranberry!" Mayor Quill barked.

"He's not *just* a cranberry. He's the *Grand* Cranberry. And every year on Hibernation Eve, he rises from the Grumpy Bog and floats through the air with his bags

of presents for everyone," said
Humphrey. He handed a piece of
paper to each townscritter.

"I don't understand why we have
to write letters, though," said Sam.

"Well, the Grand Cranberry is very busy. Therefore, it's polite for all correspondence to be in writing," explained Humphrey, holding up his own letter to the Grand Cranberry.

"So we just write to him and demand he make it snow and he will?" asked Mayor Quill.

"You might want to try a softer

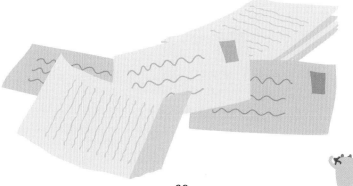

approach," said Humphrey. "Try
writing 'please.'"

"Maybe you sssshould read
ussss yourssss for an example,"
suggested Sherry.

"It's personal," said Humphrey,
hugging his letter close. But he

wasn't holding it tight enough. Sam
snatched it.

Humphrey rolled into an
embarrassed ball as Sam read.

"Dear Grand Cranberry, it's me,
Humphrey. I very much look forward
to Hibernation Eve. Thank you so

much for the necktie and clipboard you gave me last year. This year I was wondering if you would please bring me the new Flying Blind box set and a copy of *A Mammal's Guide to Becoming Mayor*? Sincerely Yours, Humphrey Hedgehog."

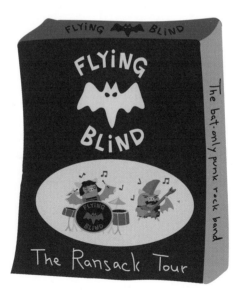

The townscritters erupted into laughter.

"Flying Blind? You actually like that noise?"

"I never took you for a punk rocker, Humphrey!"

"MAMMAL MAYOR! MAMMAL MAYOR!"

Another quill storm was brewing. Mayor Quill crumpled the blank paper in his paw and stomped his foot, alerting the others to stop laughing immediately and get busy writing letters of their own. He would deal with Humphrey's little dream of being mayor later.

"Oh, *assistant*," said the mayor, stressing the word to remind Humphrey of his role, "get me a

new piece of paper. This one is a
tad wrinkled."

Humphrey unballed himself and
dutifully handed a fresh sheet of
stationery to Mayor Quill.

"How's this?" asked Bernice,
reading from her paper. "Dearest

Grand Cranberry, please make
it snow in the Grumpy Woods. A
lot. A whole lot. It could actually

make me happy. Sincerely, Bernice

Bunny."

"That's goOOOd," said Opal.

"Yessss, it issss," said Sherry.

Mayor Quill was skeptical. All

he had written so far was the letter
D. Polite letter-writing was not his
strong suit. However, if it stopped a
party, he was willing to be as polite
as needed.

So that was that. Everyone got to work writing letters with lots of words like *please*. When they were finished, they stuffed them in envelopes.

"You'll deliver these for us?" Bernice asked Humphrey.

"Oh no! That's not how it works," said Humphrey. "Everyone who writes a letter to the Grand Cranberry must deliver it themselves to the Grumpy Bog on Hibernation Eve. Otherwise your wish won't come true."

"Absolutely NOT!" protested Mayor Quill.

Dawn Fawn stopped humming and dropped her feather duster. The thought of going to the muddy, swampy Grumpy Bog was a very scary thing for a clean freak like Dawn.

"Suit yourselves," said Humphrey. "Let me know how that fruitcake tastes."

The townscritters detested the thought of going to the Grumpy Bog. But they detested the Super

Happy Party Bears' holiday cheer even more. They voted on it and it was official.

With letters in hand, they made their way through the Grumpy Woods to enlist the help of a piece of fruit.

CHAPTER SIX

The Grumpy Bog was wet. It
was muddy. It was sticky. And
Dawn Fawn had no intention of
spending one second plopped
down in it. Therefore, when all
the other critters marched off to

the swamp, Dawn stayed back, instead focusing her attention on the heaps of confetti the bears had left behind. She wanted to get it all cleaned up before everyone returned to City Hall covered in mud. Muddy paws plus confetti was not a good mix.

When Dawn was just a young doe she believed in the Grand Cranberry. In fact, she sat with Humphrey, who was then just a little hedgehog, all night one Hibernation Eve with her special letter clutched in her hooves. The letter asked the Grand Cranberry for a dolly who could open and

shut her eyes. But Dawn awoke on
Hibernation morning surrounded
by muck and no dolly. Humphrey
insisted that the dolly must have
sunk to the bottom of the bog, so

for the next several hours, Dawn and Humphrey snorkeled in the sludge. This only resulted in getting filthier.

To make matters worse, Humphrey argued with Dawn and still insisted that the Grand Cranberry granted wishes. After all, he had asked for a new bottle of bubble bath, and as soon as he got home, his mother dunked him into the warmest, sudsiest bath ever. As for Dawn, she got a bath, too. But not her dolly.

And that is why, to this day,
Dawn battles dirt and grime in
the Grumpy Woods. "No good
can come of mess," she says, "but
unfulfilled wishes."

While lost in her memories,
Dawn furiously swept up the
mountains of confetti at City Hall.

When finished there, she followed
the trail of tinsel and glitter left by
the bears, sweeping as she went.

"CRANBERRY SCAM!
CRANBERRY SCAM!" she sang.

The harder she swept, the
more static electricity she built
up, causing the confetti to cling to

her. By the time her cleaning led her across the woods and straight up the flower-lined path of the Party Patch, she looked like a dirt-busting disco ball.

She paused on the front stoop. Through the bear-shaped door, she could hear the bustling inside—a flurry of final preparations for the Hibernation Eve celebration, a celebration that was sure to cause even more mess. Anger bubbled up inside her.

Using the end of her broom

handle like a battering ram, she
pounded on the Party Patch door,
causing it to swing wide open.

The bears stared as Dawn Fawn
entered, covered in glitter and
tinsel. She was sick of cleaning up
after everyone else. She was sick

of struggling to keep the woods
clutter-free without any thanks.

"I WANT MY DOLLY! I WANT MY
DOLLY!" she sang out with rage
before collapsing in a puddle of
tears.

CHAPTER SEVEN

Meanwhile, Humphrey Hedgehog waded right into the Grumpy Bog as the rest of the townscritters stood by the edge. They watched as Humphrey fought the suction of the mud with each step forward.

He reached the center before he realized that no one had followed.

"You know, it's rude to just demand wishes without actually making any real effort to get to know the Grand Cranberry," he called back.

"But it'ssss ssssquishy," said Sherry.

"Fine," said Humphrey. "Then kiss your wish good-bye."

The critters hesitated until one by one they reluctantly entered the bog. It seemed to gurgle and burp with each step. A *blub-blub-blub* groaned from the reeds at the far end.

"There's something alive in here," announced Squirrelly Sam.

"That's your imagination," said Mayor Quill, trying desperately to believe himself.

"Something just moved past my leg," said Sam. "Look! Did you see that?"

"Just keep walking, you furry oaf," barked Mayor Quill. "It's probably just an eel."

Sam gulped. "EEL?!" The squirrel panicked. He yanked himself from the mud and leaped across the heads of Bernice, Sherry, Opal, and

Mayor Quill until he finally came to rest on top of Humphrey. Paw-print muck dripped down the angry face of each townscritter.

"So now what doOOOO we doOOOO?" asked Opal.

"We wait," said Humphrey. "We await your good tidings, Grand Cranberry!" he called into the night air while carefully placing the stack of letters on a large boulder.

"How long do we have to stay out here?" asked Bernice.

"The Grand Cranberry does not like to be rushed," proclaimed Humphrey. "Better make yourselves comfortable."

So, that's what they did. The

townscritters made themselves
comfortable, or as comfortable as
possible when you are up to your
shoulders in oozy, gooey sludge,
leaning on your neighbor. And they
waited.

And waited.

And waited.

They watched the moon rise high
and then start its descent again.
They counted fireflies twinkling all
around them. They listened to the

lullaby of distant frog croaks. And soon their snores joined in the lullaby. That's right, with all that waiting, they fell asleep.

Several hours passed. Bernice was the first to stir. Her little nose twitched. It felt cold and icy. Thinking she was cozy in her own bed, she rolled over and tried to grab more covers, but instead she grabbed Opal's wing. Opal shrieked and flapped, spraying mud everywhere. It was then that Sam opened his eyes.

"SNOW!!!!!!!" he yelled, alerting the others, who woke up and couldn't believe their eyes.

Everything, as far as they could

see, was covered in fluffy white snow. Yup, the Grumpy Woods was having a blizzard. And the townscritters were trapped in a very frozen, very icy Grumpy Bog.

CHAPTER EIGHT

Back at the Party Patch, the bears
wrapped Dawn Fawn in their
favorite blanket and poured her
a mug of piping hot cocoa (with
extra marshmallows). Dawn
sat still, with her head down,
clutching the mug and watching

the marshmallows bobbing in the cocoa. It reminded her of sitting in the Grumpy Bog, waiting for her

wish to come true. She closed her eyes and hummed to make the thoughts go away.

"She doesn't look so good," said Mops.

"Poor thing," said Tunes, patting Dawn on the back.

Bubs was blowing his party-wisdom bubbles in the corner. "Sometimes, like the doughnut, we all feel empty inside."

Everyone oohed and aahed at his wisdom.

"So Dawn needs to be filled up with something?" asked Little Puff.

"Like raspberry jelly?" asked the littlest bear.

"Not quite," said Shades. "We

need to fill Dawn back up with

positivity!"

"And the perfect way to do that,"

said Mops, "is our pre-Hibernation celebration!"

The Party Patch erupted in cheers as the bears snapped back into party-prep mode.

"IT'S SUPER HAPPY PARTY TIME! SUPER HAPPY PARTY TIME!"

Slide to the right.

Hop to the left.

Shimmy, shimmy, shake.

Strike a pose.

115

When they were finally ready, the bears looked over their list and checked it twice.

"Decorations. Check."

"Tasty treats. Check."

"Bowls of punch. Check."

"Stacks of presents. Check."

"Wait," said the littlest bear, removing a gift marked To Dawn from the pile and handing it to her. "Dawn, the pre-Hibernation holiday is a time when friends and family come together to eat, drink, and have a party. But most important it's when we all have one extra special day in the year to express just how much we care for one another and to spread love and kindness. So this is for you."

Maybe it was the lingering scent of baking in the air. Or maybe a piece of holiday tinsel had gone

into her ear and straight to her
brain. Whatever it was, Dawn Fawn
felt woozy as
she untied the
bow and tore
the paper away
to reveal
a dolly who
could open and
shut her eyes.

Dawn hugged the
dolly tight. She may
have even smiled . . .
a little.

"Now we are all set!" exclaimed the littlest bear.

However, when the bears opened the Party Patch door, all they saw was snow. A solid wall of snow. The blizzard had quickly dropped several feet on the Grumpy Woods. It was sparkly and beautiful. But the bears were snowed in.

"What will we do now?" asked Little Puff.

"The woods are lovely, dark, and deep," said Bubs. "But we have promises to keep!"

"I think Bubs is trying to tell us that the party must go on," said Shades.

The bears didn't quite understand poetry, but they cheered anyway. In a flurry of excitement, they bundled up in hats and scarves. They created snowshoes out of dinner plates.

They broke apart chairs and tables and made skis. The snow wouldn't stop the bears from their pre-Hibernation celebration.

"But how will we carry all this through the snow?" asked Mops, looking at the stacks of presents and party supplies.

Their arms were hardly big

enough. And with mittens on, it is pretty much impossible to hold on to anything. The bears gazed around the Party Patch. Surely there was some way.

"We need a sleigh!" said Shades.

"How about the blow-up swimming pool?" asked Jacks.

"Perfect!" cheered the bears. They loaded up the pool with all their holiday goodies. Yet, there was one problem. Even twelve incredibly positive bears could not pull the makeshift sleigh. It was simply too heavy.

That's when they saw their

answer. Dawn Fawn could pull the sleigh. And although most of the glitter and confetti had finally fallen off her, there remained a big glob on her nose. Her nose glowed like a lightbulb. Her nose worked as a perfect headlight to pull their Super Happy Holiday Sleigh through the blizzard.

So, the bears asked, "Dawn Fawn, with your nose aglow, won't you pull our sleigh through the snow?"

CHAPTER NINE

Now to say that Dawn Fawn agreed
right away would not be entirely
true. You see, she *was* feeling a
little weak after her tirade and so
her defenses were a *little* down.
But it would take a lot more than
that to convince her.

There was a lot of "I'm not a reindeer" and "pretty please" back and forth. But when she looked into the eyes of her little dolly, her heart seemed to grow three times.

She walked over to the blow-up pool sleigh and tucked her dolly securely into the front of her apron before placing the harness over her head.

"IT'S SUPER HAPPY DAWN TIME! SUPER HAPPY DAWN TIME!" the bears cheered.

"Wait!" said Little Puff. She

ran over to her craft supplies. A few seconds later she presented Dawn with a beautiful festive set of reindeer antlers. "Gotta look the part."

The Super Happy Holiday Sleigh slowly made its way across the Grumpy Woods. Of course, Dawn knew that no one would be at City Hall, so she led the bears to the Grumpy Bog, where they found several grumpy icicles.

The townscritters were relieved to be rescued. With a few sips of the bears' hot cocoa they were warmed up enough to be free from the ice and snow.

"I never thought I would be sssso happy to ssssee you all,"

said Sherry as she slithered aboard the sleigh and right into an ugly sweater.

In fact, the ugly sweaters were welcomed by all the townscritters, who were still chilled.

"I told you the Grand Cranberry would grant our wishes," said Humphrey.

"What are *you* wearing?" Sam asked Dawn, eyeing her antlers.

Once everyone was safely delivered to City Hall, Mayor Quill decreed that no one was ever to spend the night in the Grumpy Bog again . . . without blankets and space heaters.

The Super Happy Party Bears presented their not-so-boring gifts. Sherry's ssssnake ssssock doll and Dawn's dolly got along from the start.

All the friends they sent

invitations to showed up for the

celebration. (Well, except the

beavers.) Stan the bumblebee

arrived and brought some samples

of his newest honey line from his

Getsy shop. The Puffy Cheeks
and the Twitchy Tails danced the
Nutcracker—literally cracking nuts.
Wallace Woodpecker even showed

up and used his wood-carving
skills to fix those square wheels
on the mayor's train. It was the
best holiday party ever.

Soon, with full bellies and full hearts, the Super Happy Party Bears snuggled up for a cozy hibernation together.

And you know what? The townscritters snuggled up, too.

They were feeling just a *little less grumpy*. THE END.

ABOUT THE AUTHOR

In previous chapters, Marcie Colleen has been a teacher, an actress, and a nanny, but now she spends her days writing children's books! She lives in her very own Party Patch, Headquarters of Fun, with her husband and their mischievous sock monkey in San Diego, California. Occasionally, there are even doughnuts. This is her first chapter book series.

Don't Miss the other SUPER HAPPY PARTY BEARS Books

SUPER HAPPY PARTY BEARS
GNAWING AROUND
MARCIE COLLEEN

SUPER HAPPY PARTY BEARS
KNOCK KNOCK on WOOD
MARCIE COLLEEN

SUPER HAPPY PARTY BEARS
STAYING A HIVE
MARCIE COLLEEN

SUPER HAPPY PARTY BEARS
GOING NUTS
MARCIE COLLEEN

SUPER HAPPY PARTY BEARS
BAT to THE BONE
MARCIE COLLEEN

SUPER HAPPY PARTY BEARS
THE JITTERBUG
MARCIE COLLEEN